Moby Dick

Moby Dick

Herman Melville

**Retold by
Bernice Selden**

**Illustrated by
Gary Gianni**

Troll

Library of Congress Cataloging-in-Publication Data

Selden, Bernice.
　Moby Dick.

　　Summary: A young seaman joins the crew of the
fanatical Captain Ahab in pursuit of the white
whale Moby Dick.
　　[1. Whaling—Fiction.　　2. Whales—Fiction.
3. Sea stories]　I. Gianni, Gary, ill.　　II. Melville,
Herman, 1819-1891.　Moby Dick.　　III. Title.
PZ7.S45687Mo　　　1988　　[Fic]　　87-16788
ISBN 0-8167-1207-7 (lib. bdg.)
ISBN 0-8167-7478-1 (pbk.)

This edition published in 2002.

Call me Ishmael.

Many years ago, having no money in my pockets and nothing much to do, I thought I would go sailing in a ship. I wanted to see the watery parts of the world and to visit strange and interesting places.

At that time every healthy young man was eager to go to sea, even though life on a ship could be harsh and cruel. A sailor often faced danger, and even death. But what better adventure could a man have while getting paid at the same time? What better opening was there into a world of mystery and wonder?

More than anything, I wanted to hunt the whale—that mysterious monster who was as tall as a mountain and whose breath rose in spouts of mist that were higher than treetops.

So I stuffed a shirt or two into my old traveling bag and left my home in the city of New York. I headed for the port of New Bedford, Massachusetts. My mind was made up to sail to sea from Nantucket. To reach Nantucket, I had to take a packet boat from New Bedford.

I arrived in New Bedford on a very cold, rainy December night. The rain lashed at me as I hurried through the streets, looking for a place to sleep. Near the waterfront I came upon

a house with a swinging sign on it that read "The Spouter Inn—Peter Coffin."

"I must have a place to spend the night," I told the man who appeared at the door. He was the landlord.

"Ah, I don't have a single room . . ." he began to say. "But wait! You wouldn't object to sharing a bed with a harpooner, would you? A good man, and he pays on time. Why, I hear he can lance a whale that's halfway around the other side of the earth."

"I don't like to sleep two in a bed," I said, "but I don't want to spend the night going from inn to inn. It's far too cold for that. So lead me to it."

Up the stairs we went and into a small room that was cold as a clam. I got into a bed that was big enough for four harpooners, and soon slipped into a light doze.

Suddenly a tall, dark man entered the room. His hair was done up in a knot on top of his head, and his body and face were covered with tattoos.

I made a sound, startling the stranger. "Who you?" he said in broken English. "You no speak, I kill." He held what looked like a small tomahawk in his hand.

"Help! Landlord! Peter Coffin!" I shouted.

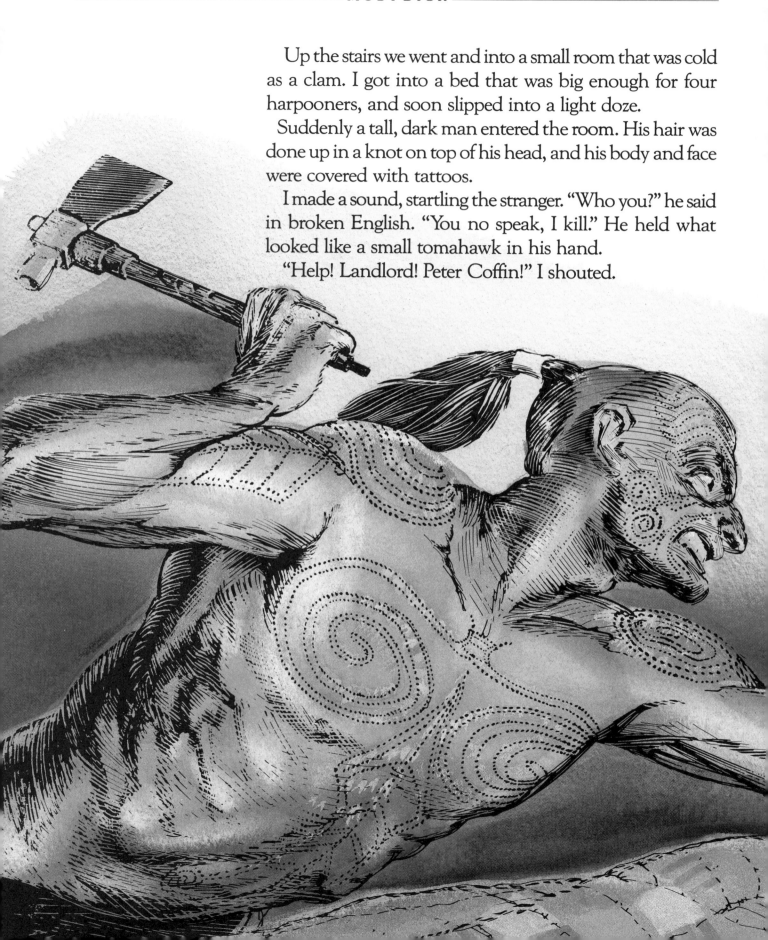

The landlord came, holding a light. He laughed when he saw how frightened I was. "Don't be afraid. This is only Queequeg. He is a native of the South Seas and his father is king of a tribe there. Queequeg wouldn't harm you."

"Stop grinning," I said. "You didn't tell me that the harpooner was a savage."

Little did I know then that this "savage" and I would soon be friends. Queequeg turned out to be gentle and kind.

The next evening, we shared stories of our lives. Queequeg pulled out his pipe to share a smoke with me. His pipe turned out to be the tomahawk that had frightened me the night before. Then he pressed his forehead to mine, which was the way the men in his country decided to be friends for life. He took thirty silver coins out of a pouch he had and made me take half of them. It was then that we decided to ship out together.

As I walked the dock at Nantucket the following morning, one ship caught my eye. It was called *Pequod*, named after a tribe of Massachusetts Indians who hunted whales many years before.

The ship was weather-stained from traveling through storms on four oceans. Its masts stood up straight and high. And the bow was shaped like a whale's jaw and had real whale's teeth decorating it.

The owner, a very old sailor himself, was sitting on deck in a strange sort of tent pitched behind the mast. He signed me on for the next voyage.

"I have a friend who wants to ship out too," I told him.

"Has he ever whaled any?" the owner asked.

"He's killed more whales than you or I can count."

"Well, then bring him along," he said gruffly.

But when I came back with Queequeg, the owner said he wanted no savages aboard.

Queequeg jumped into a whaleboat hanging from the ship's side. Then, holding up a harpoon, he called down, "You see small drop of tar on water there? Well, then, suppose tar is whale eye."

And with that, he shot the harpoon over the head of the owner and across the deck. It landed smack in the center of the drop of tar on the water. The spot of tar disappeared. "Whale dead," said Queequeg.

"Quick, get the ship's papers," said the owner to one of the hands. "We must have Hedgehog—I mean Quohog—I mean Queequeg, whatever his name is. And he will get more money than ever was given a harpooner out of Nantucket."

11

For several days Queequeg and I watched the *Pequod* being loaded. There were new sails, yards of canvas, coils of rope for the rigging, and many empty barrels for whale oil. Quite a few housekeeping items were needed for this three-year journey, including pans, knives, forks, and beds. Also taken on board were beef, bread, water, and fuel. Back and forth went the men, fetching and carrying.

At last the anchor was up, the sails were set, and out to sea we headed.

We found out that the captain's name was Ahab. But where was this captain? He disappeared into his cabin as soon as he came on board. For all we knew, the sailors at the watch could have been the commanders.

We sailed during a particularly cold Christmas. Skies were stormy, and the ocean was black and cold. For many days I came up on deck hoping to catch a glimpse of our captain, but there was no sign of him.

The order of command after Ahab was Chief Mate Starbuck, Second Mate Stubb, and Third Mate Flask. When there were whales to be caught, each of these men was in charge of his own whaleboat, with his own crew and harpooner. Queequeg was Starbuck's harpooner. Tashtego, an Indian from Massachusetts, was the harpooner in Stubb's boat, and Daggoo, an African, was the one who did the harpooning in Flask's boat.

Starbuck was a tall, lean man of thirty. He was strong and calm, but in his eyes you could see the horrors he had witnessed at sea. It was the sea that had claimed the lives of both his father and his brother.

Stubb was a happy-go-lucky fellow who could be heard humming tunes even during the most deadly encounters with whales. He smoked a pipe constantly and kept a rack of them ready and loaded, like guns, at his fingertips.

Flask was a short, stout young fellow. He was out to kill as many of the great whales as possible, as if each one were his own personal enemy.

There was another sailor named Fedallah, who seemed to be on board only to whisper advice to the captain and be his first oarsman.

As we were passing southward one gloomy day, away from the bitter winter of New England, Ahab finally stepped out onto the quarterdeck. Shivers ran through me when I saw him. A long, yellow scar ran from the gray hair of his head, down one side of his deeply sunburned skin, and disappeared into his shirt collar. It looked as if the scar ran the length of his whole body. Grimly Ahab stood there, peering out to sea.

But what made my hair stand on end was the sight of the captain's one false leg. It was made of ivory that had been finely carved from the jaw of a sperm whale. I saw that two holes had been drilled at either end of the deck where the tip of his ivory leg could rest and not slip.

As the days passed, Ahab said very little and looked as though some mighty worry weighed him down. He often spent the night pacing the deck, disturbing the sleep of the men below with the pounding of his peg leg.

One evening Ahab, his eyes sparkling, came on deck. He placed his ivory leg in its accustomed hole and ordered Starbuck to summon all the sailors.

"Sir, is there some emergency?" Starbuck asked.

"Ask no questions," Ahab said.

When the company was assembled, Ahab held up a Spanish doubloon, a gold piece worth sixteen dollars. That was a great deal of money at the time.

With a hammer in his hand, poised to nail the doubloon to the mast, Ahab shouted out, "Whoever finds a white whale with a crooked jaw and three holes in his body, he shall have this gold piece, my boys!"

"Hurrah! Hurrah!" cried the seamen.

"It's a white whale, I say," cried Ahab. "Look sharp for white water, and if ye but see a bubble, sing out."

"Captain, is that the white whale they call Moby Dick?" asked Tashtego.

"And has he one, two, three—oh, a good many harpoon-iron in his hide?" Queequeg said, trying to describe the sight.

"Aye, Queequeg," said the captain, "that's the whale. The harpoons are twisted in him like corkscrews."

"Captain," said Starbuck, "I have heard of this whale. But wasn't it this very whale, Moby Dick, that took off your leg?"

"Yes," said Ahab bitterly. "It was he that brought me to this dead stump I stand on now. It was the terrible white whale that crippled me forever and a day. And I will chase him over all the seven seas until he spouts black blood—until he is forever gone!"

"God keep me! God keep us all!" muttered Starbuck under his breath, shaking his head sadly. "It is madness to be so enraged at a dumb beast."

But Ahab did not hear him.

Duringthe long days that followed, the *Pequod* sailed
around whole continents. Ahab plotted the course with a
pencil on old sea charts. It was a path that would lead the
Pequod through four oceans.

The ship sailed into storms so wild that they sometimes
tore the sails to rags. Then, at other times, the seas were so
quiet that I, Ishmael, could barely keep awake at my watch.
Pleasant dreams beckoned.

Finally the *Pequod* sailed into the straits of Sunda, in the
China Seas. The ship passed between the islands of Java and
Sumatra. This was the gateway to a world of spices, silks,
and jewels, of gold and ivory.

We were getting close to the waters where sperm whales, and particularly Moby Dick, might be found. The sailors who were lookouts were told to keep alert.

One day the ship was sailing close to one of the islands. The lookouts could see its green palmy cliffs in the distance. The scent of fresh cinnamon was in the air.

Suddenly a shout was heard from one of the lookouts. Not one whale, nor two, nor three, but a whole army of whales was coming toward us. The white mists emerging from the whales' spouts were like so many cheerful chimneys.

"Aloft there!" called Captain Ahab. "Rig the buckets to wet the sails!"

All hands got busy. The harpooners cheered as they jumped into the whaleboats and set off from the ship. Quickly they closed in on the whales.

Queequeg plunged his harpoon into the side of a whale. It pitched and tossed, becoming tangled in the harpoon rope. "Line! Line!" Queequeg shouted to his shipmates.

Again the whale was speared, this time in the tail with a cutting blade. The now twice-wounded whale swam off, thrashing violently. As it struggled, the harpoon and the cutting blade lines became twisted together. Then, the cutting blade came loose. And so with each whip of the whale's tail, the cutting blade was hurled about wildly, slashing and wounding other whales nearby.

Yet, with whales so thick around the *Pequod* that it could barely move, only one whale was caught. It took many harpoons to kill this giant creature. Finally, in a stream of blood that reddened the sea around them, the whale shook fitfully and died.

This unfortunate creature would now be turned into strips of fat called blubber. These strips would be boiled in pots as large as the sailors themselves and converted into whale oil.

The oil was stored in casks that would be brought back to the United States and sold by the ship's owners. One whale alone could yield fifty such casks of oil, or nearly ten tons, and most whalers brought back far more. Whale oil had many uses, but mostly it provided light for the lamps in homes.

As we sailed on in quest of Moby Dick, it was discovered that some of the casks on the *Pequod* were leaking. The leaks had to be found and stopped. My friend Queequeg, who was nimble and willing, was chosen to go deep into the hold to find the faulty casks. It was dark and cold down in the ship's hold. Queequeg broke into a sweat while he worked, and then got chilled.

The chill turned to fever soon after, and for days he lay in his sleeping hammock. The fever only got worse, as I watched his body get thinner and his cheekbones sharper. Then his eyes glazed over, as if the spirit of life were leaving him. We gave him up for a dying man.

Queequeg had heard that Nantucket whalemen often asked to be placed in canoes made of dark wood after they died. The canoes were then floated gently out to sea. That was not so different from the way the dead were treated in the South Seas, where he was born. His voice raspy with fever, Queequeg asked the ship's carpenter to make him a canoe of dark wood.

But no sooner was the last nail hammered in and the lid fitted over this unusual coffin-canoe than Queequeg suddenly got better. When he was well again, he used the canoe as a sea chest. He carved fancy designs on the lid, somewhat like the tattoos on his body.

The *Pequod* was now nearing the Japanese whaling grounds, close to where Moby Dick might be found. The seas were calm, too calm. The men were uneasy, especially when they heard an unearthly wailing at night, like the cries of dying men.

One morning the lookout fell from his post high up on the mast. Before we could get to the man, he sank below the surface of the sea. We threw the life buoy after him. But for some reason, this life buoy filled with water and went down right after the sailor, as if to provide him a pillow at the bottom of the ocean. Fear of approaching bad luck went through us all.

Queequeg later suggested that his canoe might serve as a life buoy, since there was no other.

"A life buoy made out of a coffin!" Starbuck said. He had an odd look on his face.

"Why not?" said Flask. "There is nothing else we can use, and a ship must have a life buoy."

"Carpenter!" called Starbuck. "Rig this canoe into a life buoy right away. And no questions, if you please!"

Days afterward, Ahab dreamed that he had died and a big hearse had come to carry him away. He told Fedallah about this dream.

"Have I not told you, old man," said Fedallah, "that you will have neither a hearse nor a coffin?"

"Ah, there are no hearses for those who die at sea," said Ahab, brightening.

"But you will see two hearses before you die," predicted Fedallah. "The first will be one not made by human hands. The second will be made of wood grown in America."

"Are you saying that I shall kill Moby Dick and yet live?" asked Ahab eagerly.

"It will take a rope to kill you," Fedallah said mysteriously.

The tired, old captain leaned over the side of the ship, looking at the waves. There was a mild wind, and a calm sky. The air was sweet and smelled almost like a meadow.

Ahab's face was a mass of wrinkles. His eyes glowed like live coals. He thought about the forty years he had spent at sea. They were hard and painful years of separation from family and friends. A tear fell from his eye.

Starbuck watched him from a distance. Finally he gathered up the courage to say, "Oh, my captain, noble soul! Let us go home! Why must we give chase to that hated Moby Dick? He is a creature that brings nought but harm to all who encounter him. Think of our wives and children waiting for us these long years we have been away. I beg of you, let me turn this ship around."

"No!" said Ahab, his features hardening to a frown. "I must do what even my heart tells me not to. We must go on!"

Later that day, a typhoon burst from the sky and struck the *Pequod*. By evening, the sky filled with thunder. Many of the sails were torn and fluttering in the violent wind. At every flash of lightning, Starbuck would glance aloft to see if the ship had been damaged again.

After a series of flashes, rolls of thunder were heard overhead. At the same instant, a voice pierced the darkness. The voice was Ahab's. He was working his way toward the ship's mast, motioning toward the sky.

Looking up, we saw three masts had caught fire at the top.

"Have mercy on us," said Stubb.

"Aye, men, aye!" cried Ahab. "Look upon this sign and mark it well. The white flame lights the way to the white whale, Moby Dick!"

Starbuck then pointed to the bow of Ahab's whaleboat. A tall flame of fire was shooting up from the tip of Ahab's harpoon. Starbuck grasped Ahab by the arm. "We must stop! This is an ill voyage. Ill begun, ill continued. Let me square the sails, turn around, and make a fair wind homewards."

But Captain Ahab ignored his pleas. With the flaming harpoon now in his hands, Ahab turned to his crew. "All your oaths to hunt the white whale are as binding as mine.

Old Ahab is bound—heart, soul, body, lungs, and life. Just so you know. Now, I blow out the last fear!" And with one blast of breath, Ahab snuffed the flame on his harpoon.

Ahab then ordered the sails to be let out. We made our way through the typhoon to an unknown destiny. I wondered, had our own captain become a force of evil? It seemed even nature was against him.

Among the ships the *Pequod* soon came across were the *Samuel Enderby* and the *Rachel*. The *Samuel Enderby* flew the flag of England. The captain, a tall man tanned by his months at sea, stood on the deck. One arm of his blue jacket hung loosely at his side.

"Ahoy! Have ye seen the white whale?" asked Ahab as he came aboard the other ship.

"Look," said the *Samuel Enderby* captain, holding up a false arm made of whalebone. "My arm got caught in a harpoon when I was trying to catch a bouncing great whale with a milk-white head and hump. He sailed away at great speed."

"It must be him! Moby Dick!" cried Ahab in great excitement. "Did you try to find him again?"

"Do you think I am mad? I lost one arm already!"

"Which way was he heading?" asked Ahab.

"He was heading east," replied the other captain.

No sooner did he hear this than Ahab departed, a man possessed by one demonic wish.

Not many days later, the *Rachel* came bearing down on the *Pequod* bringing bad news.

The captain of the *Rachel* seemed about to say something when Ahab called out, "Have ye seen the white whale?"

"Aye, I saw him yesterday. And have *you* seen a small whaleboat adrift?" The *Rachel* captain had now climbed to the deck of the *Pequod*.

"Where was the whale?" asked Ahab. "Not killed?"

"But you do not understand," said Captain Gardiner. "One of my boats is lost. And my *own boy*, only a lad of twelve, was in that boat. I beg you, help me find him. You *must* help me!"

"His son!" said Stubb. "Oh, it's his son he's lost. Captain Ahab, we must save that boy."

Ahab stood like a rock. "Captain Gardiner, I will not do it. Moby Dick is close at hand. Even now I am losing time!" And with that, Ahab told the captain to leave.

From that moment on, Ahab never left the deck. He was waiting for the sight of his mortal enemy, Moby Dick. He ate and slept on deck, with Fedallah standing beside him.

For days nothing was seen. Then...a shout broke the silence. "There she blows! There she blows!" Ahab yelled. "A hump like a snow hill. It is the white whale!"

The men rushed to the rigging to see the famous whale they had been pursuing all around the world. Moby Dick was a mile away, but his hump and silvery spouting could clearly be seen.

"And did none of you see it before I did?" asked Ahab of the men around him.

"I saw him almost that same instant, Captain Ahab, and I cried out," said Tashtego.

"Not at the same instant, though," said Ahab. "No, the doubloon is mine. Fate reserved the doubloon for me. None of you could have sighted the white whale first. Only I."

Soon all the boats but Starbuck's were dropped and all the boat sails set. The boats came upon their foe slowly, and the ocean grew calm as the men steered closer.

White birds were flying toward Ahab's boat now. They wheeled round and round it, crying out as they circled. The birds were peering down into the sea, but Ahab could not see anything below the water's surface.

Ahab looked more closely into the water. He saw a white spot rising upward from below and growing larger as it rose. Suddenly it broke through the surface, revealing two long, crooked rows of teeth. It was Moby Dick's open mouth! The white whale shook the boat as a cat shakes a mouse. Ahab tried to seize the huge head with his bare hands, but the sides of the whaleboat bent in and collapsed. Those jaws, like enormous shears, bit the craft completely in half! We were dumped into the sea and swam back to the *Pequod*. Then the whale drifted away, ending the first day of the chase.

The next day, Moby Dick burst into view in a mountain of dazzling foam. Again, three whaleboats went out after him, with Ahab's boat in the middle.

But no sooner had we lowered away and started the chase than Moby Dick turned and headed straight for us. Captain Ahab, cheering us on, said he'd meet the white whale head-to-head. But before that could happen, Moby Dick suddenly veered and rushed among the boats with open jaws and lashing tail. All of us hurled our harpoons at him. Yet they seemed to have no effect as the whale tried to smash each boat into splinters.

For the most part, we managed to escape his crunching jaws and flapping tail. But Moby Dick was so powerful and quick that, as he pulled away, the boats got caught in the harpoon ropes and were overturned. Once more we had to swim back to the ship.

When we were all on board, we learned that Fedallah, Ahab's companion, was missing!

"Shall we keep chasing this murderous creature?" Starbuck asked, clearly afraid. "Shall we be dragged by him to the bottom of the sea?"

"I must go on," said Ahab. "It is fate that I serve. I vow that tomorrow will be Moby Dick's last day of life."

The morning of the third day was fair and calm, eerily so. Ahab sent out the whaleboats, even though sharks were all around. The boats had not gone very far when there was a signal from the mastheads. Ahab now knew that the whale had dived below. The water around them slowly swelled in broad circles, then quickly heaved upward. A low rumbling sound from the water's depths could be heard. Everyone held their breaths. Again, the huge form of Moby Dick surfaced. This time the white whale was maddened by his pain and churned his giant tail among the boats. He destroyed two but left Ahab's boat untouched.

Suddenly one of the oarsmen cried out, "Look!" He was pointing to the body of Fedallah, which was lashed to the whale by his own harpoon rope. Here was the first part of Fedallah's prediction: a hearse not made by human hands!

Ahab gasped, then rose to his feet. "Face to face, I meet you this third time, Moby Dick!" he shouted. His boat was so close to the whale that he was actually within the shower of mist thrown off by the spout.

The white whale began to slow down. But Captain Ahab pressed on, gliding over the waves in pursuit. All the while, sharks bit at the oars. Soon the blades became jagged with teeth marks.

"Forget them, men! Pull on!" Ahab shouted. "The blades will last long enough."

Ahab was standing erect in the prow of the boat, a harpoon in his hands. The boat moved up alongside the huge whale. Then Ahab lifted his arms high and plunged the harpoon with all his might into the side of Moby Dick.

Enraged, Moby Dick focused on the *Pequod* itself as if the ship were the cause of his trouble. He bore down on the ship and smashed into its side with his immense forehead amid a fiery shower of foam. Within a few moments the *Pequod* was dashed to pieces and sinking. Here was Fedallah's second prophecy: a hearse made of wood grown in America!

"The ship! The ship!" cried one of Ahab's oarsmen, wide-eyed with fear.

Moby Dick turned and charged Ahab's whaleboat again. Ahab hurled one more harpoon at the whale. Moby Dick lurched and the rope of Ahab's harpoon wound around his own neck. His body shot out of the boat and into the sea. Fedallah's third prophecy had come true: It had taken a rope to kill Ahab!

The weight of the *Pequod* began pulling it down under the sea in a deep, cone-shaped whirlpool. The water churned with tremendous force and noise, as even the smallest splinter of the once-proud ship began disappearing from view.

With horror I watched the ship go round and round, then slip under forever. Luckily, I was treading water far enough away from the whirlpool's center that I was not drawn in with the others.

I, Ishmael, was the only one to survive. And as I tried to keep my head above water, the life buoy of Queequeg's coffin suddenly surfaced. It drifted toward me and I climbed onto it. For almost a whole day and night, the coffin of my now-departed friend kept me afloat.

On the second day, I caught sight of a sail far off in the distance. As it drew nearer, I saw it was the sail of the good ship *Rachel*. It was still cruising the waters, searching for the lost whaleboat bearing the captain's son. In its search for its missing children, the ship found only me, an orphan.

And so it was I alone who lived to tell this story of the *Pequod* and Ahab. It is a sad story of a captain's hunt through the world's great oceans to kill the creature that would, in the end, kill him.